Clifford
GETS A JOB

Story and pictures by Norman Bridwell

SCHOLASTIC INC.

New York   Toronto   London   Auckland   Sydney
Mexico City   New Delhi   Hong Kong   Buenos Aires

To Bridget Mary, Deirdre, and Vera Maura

ISBN-13: 978-0-590-44296-1
ISBN-10: 0-590-44296-1

42   8/0

Printed in the U.S.A.   23

Hello—

I'm Emily Elizabeth.

If you don't live on my street,
you may not know me . . .

. . . or my dog Clifford.

He's a lot of fun to play with.

There is only one bad thing
about Clifford.

He eats a lot of dog food.
And a lot of dog food
costs a lot of money.

We were spending all our
money for dog food.
Mother and Daddy didn't
know what to do.
"We will have to send
Clifford away," they said.

Clifford didn't want to go away.
He made up his mind to get a job
and pay for his own dog food.

He decided to join the circus.
Good Old Clifford.

The circus man liked Clifford.
Clifford got the job.

But they put him in the side show.
He just sat there.
And people just looked at him.
Clifford wanted to do something.

He peeked into a tent.

He saw little dogs doing tricks.

Clifford wanted to do tricks too.

So he ran into the tent and he tried
to jump through the hoop—
just like the little dogs.

It didn't work.

In the next ring Clifford saw
a little dog riding on a pony.

Clifford thinks he can do anything a little dog can do.

But he can't.

The circus man was angry.
He asked Clifford to leave.

"Don't worry," I said.
"You can get another job."

So we went to see a farmer.

The farmer thought Clifford
would be a good farm dog.
He said Clifford could
work for him.

First Clifford rounded up the cows.

Then Clifford brought home
a wagon full of hay.
He was doing so well . . .

And then he saw a rat
running to the barn.
Clifford knew that rats on
a farm are very bad!

So Clifford chased the rat.

Clifford and I started home.

We felt very bad.

Everything had gone wrong.

Suddenly a car came speeding past us.

And right behind it came a police car.
They were chasing robbers.

Clifford took a short cut
through the woods—

—and caught the robbers.

I was very proud.
The Chief of Police
offered Clifford a job
as a police dog.

Now Clifford goes to
work every day.
They don't pay him money.
But...

. . . every week they send
Clifford a lot of dog food.
So now we can keep him.
Isn't that wonderful?
Good Old Clifford.